SOGG
and the
Mystery

M

For those children who have yet to find the ship of their dreams.
PM

For my son, Ben, who really is a diver.
MF

First published in Great Britain in 2013 by Mabecron Books Ltd, 42 Drake Circus, Plymouth, Devon PL4 8AB. All rights reserved

Typeset in Sabon
Designed by Peter Bennett

10 9 8 7 6 5 4 3 2 1

ISBN 978 09572 5602 6

Printed and bound in China

SOGGY
and the
Mystery

Philip Moran
illustrated by
Michael Foreman

Soggy and Jack were on the pier fishing for crabs when, suddenly, the lifeboat hooter sounded sending all the seagulls of the town squawking into the air.

The lifeboat rumbled down the slipway into the water.

'What's up?' Jack yelled to the Coxswain as the lifeboat passed the end of the pier.

'A ship reported in trouble,' the Coxswain shouted. 'Back soon I hope.'

Then the lifeboat vanished as a thick mist rolled in from the sea.

The mist soon covered the whole town and Soggy and Jack felt lonely in an invisible world. They were much happier when Grandfather and the old Sea Captain joined them on the end of the pier.

'Thought you boys could do with a snack,' said Grandfather, opening up a packet of bacon sandwiches. 'Try a bit o'bacon on your line Soggy. Crabs can't resist a bit o'bacon!'

S uddenly the Captain let out a shout and started dancing wildly up and down. The lifeboat was returning out of the mist and behind it was the most amazing sight.

It was like a great ghost ship, with broken masts and tattered flapping sails like the wings of an ancient sea bird.

'That's my ship!' the Captain shouted. 'My old ship, the Mystery!'
As the lifeboat towed it closer, they could see the peeling paint and barnacle covered hull. The old ship had drifted across the oceans of the world for many a year.

'What a sorry state you're in old girl,' the Captain sighed.
'Well she does look bad now,' said Grandfather. 'But with help and hard work we will make her shipshape again Captain.'

And help there was aplenty. There was great excitement in the town and everyone had turned up to pull the sad weather beaten sailing ship to the mooring posts by the old inn.

Everyone set to and barnacles were scraped carefully into buckets, paint was brought and canvas was cut and stitched for the great sails.

'Just like the good old days!' the town's old folk cried. 'When we all helped each other!'

Timber was gathered for shaping new masts.... but the one thing they could not afford was the copper needed to cover the bottom of the ship to prevent barnacles and wood eating weevils from returning.

Soggy wondered, just where they might find this important and expensive material.

Turquoise the mermaid swam in on the high tide having heard of their problem. 'Copper, you say? I know where there is some copper.... out there on the old 'Railway' wreck.'

'Of course!' Grandfather cried. 'You remember Soggy, when we first met.... when Jack and I rescued you.... you were floating over a wrecked ship. It's called the 'Railway' wreck because it was taking railway engines to France in the First World War. It was sunk by an enemy submarine.'

'Wow!' said Soggy. 'What a story, but how can we get the copper?'

'Well,' said Grandfather. 'I am too old but perhaps Jack, you and Soggy could dive for the copper. I think we might be able to borrow some diving gear from the Museum.'

Soggy was not too happy about this suggestion, not being that fond of water let alone diving!

Thankfully Jack piped up and said, 'No need for that, my big brother Ben has just become a deep sea diver. I am sure he will help us.'

Next morning much to Soggy's relief, Ben turned up with his diving gear and they all set off in Grandfather's boat to the site of the wreck.

Ben and Turquoise went down, down, deep onto the wreck.

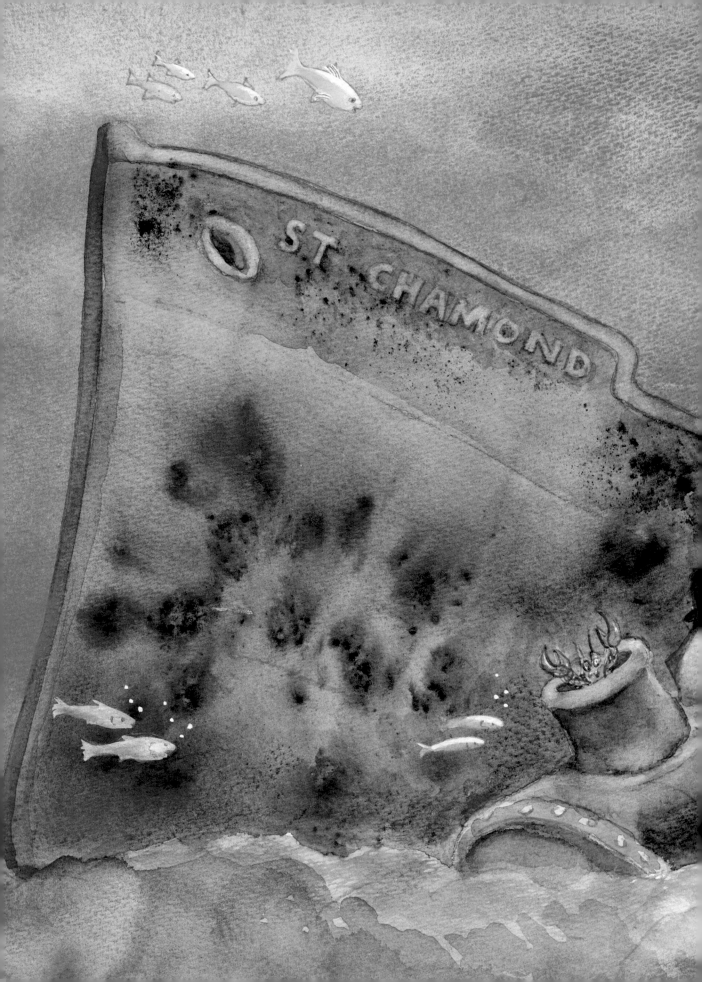

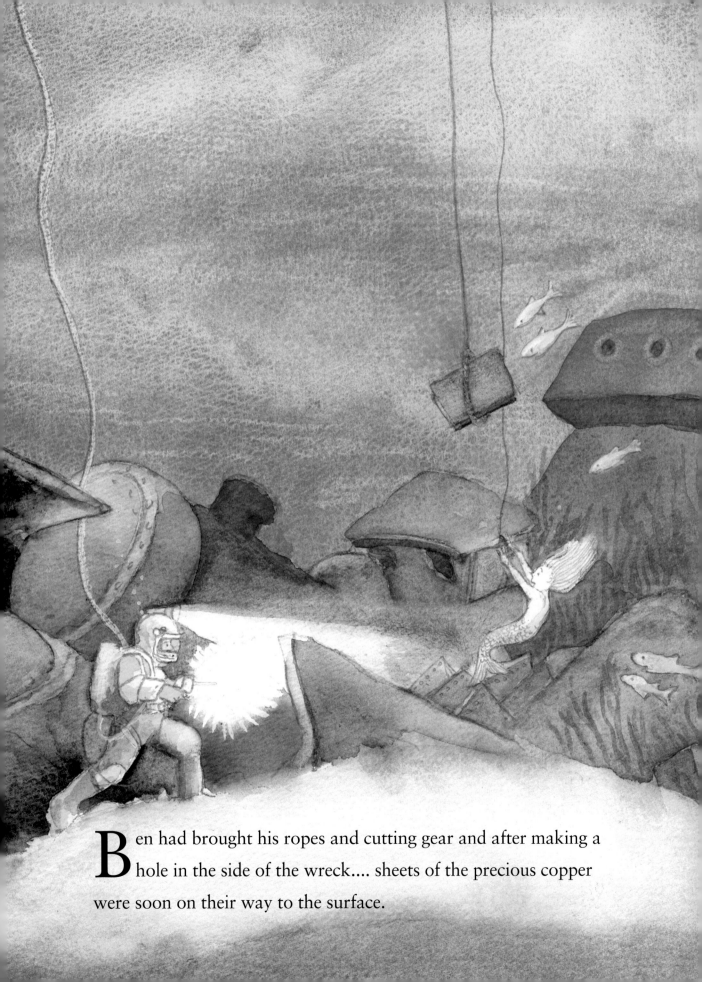

Ben had brought his ropes and cutting gear and after making a hole in the side of the wreck.... sheets of the precious copper were soon on their way to the surface.

A fleet of local boats came to help carry the copper back to the harbour.

The old songs were sung and the old skills recalled. Day by day the Mystery was being transformed into the proud and beautiful ship of the old Captain's dreams.

However Soggy still felt something was missing. He had lately been looking at pictures of old sailing ships in the town library.

'Of course!' he suddenly said. 'A figurehead!'

'You're right,' said Grandfather. 'Every sailing ship should have a figurehead to guide and protect the crew.' He turned to the old Captain.... 'What has happened to the figurehead?'

'Never had one,' said the Captain, 'not in all the time I sailed on her.'

'Why not?' asked Soggy.

'Nobody knows.' said the Captain, 'that's why she is called the Mystery.'

Soggy, a frequent visitor to the library, knew just where to look, and it was not long before he found exactly what he needed. A mysterious legend of how the town got its name.

'Long, long ago,' he told Grandfather, 'An Irish Princess called St Ia hoped to sail to Cornwall with her friends but got left behind and was very unhappy. Through her tears she saw a small leaf floating on the sea. She touched it with her staff to make it sink. Much to her surprise, it grew bigger and bigger until it was large enough to carry her safely to Cornwall.'

'Well done Soggy!' said Grandfather, 'St Ia will be a perfect figurehead.'

The local wood carver was an old friend of Grandfather's and he quickly set to work and made a fine figurehead, which they secured to the bow of the Mystery.

All the townsfolk gathered to watch Grandfather add the finishing touch to the now beautiful ship. They all clapped and cheered when they saw his handiwork. Painted in gold, it said very simply,

'MYSTERY'

St Ia.

At high tide the great sails were hoisted and the Mystery sailed majestically across the harbour to moor at the end of the pier.

The old Captain thanked everyone for making his ship so beautiful again.... and with a tear in his eye, he said, 'And now early to bed. Tomorrow we pick the crew and store the ship ready for our next adventure!'

S oggy felt he was too excited to sleep.
He could see Grandfather studying his old charts.
It was like the whole world was spread out before him.

Soggy closed his eyes.... and began to dream!

Goodbye!
And I will be
back soon with
another story.